SELECTED ENSEMBLE SONATAS

Recent Researches in the Music of the Baroque Era is one of four quarterly series (Middle Ages and Early Renaissance; Renaissance; Baroque Era; Classical Era) which make public the early music that is being brought to light in the course of current musicological research.

Each volume is devoted to works by a single composer or in a single genre of composition, chosen because of their potential interest to scholars and performers, and prepared for publication according to the standards that govern the making of all reliable historical editions.

Subscribers to this series, as well as patrons of subscribing institutions, are invited to apply for information about the "Copyright-Sharing Policy" of A-R Editions, Inc., under which the contents of this volume may be reproduced free of charge for performance use.

Correspondence should be addressed:

A-R Editions, Inc.
315 West Gorham Street
Madison, Wisconsin 53703

Dario Castello

SELECTED ENSEMBLE SONATAS

Part II

Edited by Eleanor Selfridge-Field

A-R EDITIONS, INC. · MADISON

Copyright © 1977, A-R Editions, Inc.

ISSN 0484-0828 *(Recent Researches in the Music of the Baroque Era)*

ISBN 0-89579-090-4 (Set, Parts I and II—Volumes XXIII and XXIV)
ISBN 0-89579-092-0 (Part II—Volume XXIV)

Library of Congress Cataloging in Publication Data:

Castello, Dario, fl. 1621-1644.
    [Sonate concertate in stilo moderno. Selections]
    Selected ensemble sonatas.

    (Recent researches in the music of the baroque era ;
v. 23-24 ISSN 0484-0828)
    Includes bibliographical references.
    CONTENTS: pt. 1. Sonatas from Sonate concertate,
book I (1621): Sonata 3 for two treble instruments.
Sonata 5 for treble instrument and trombone. Sonata 9
for two violins and bassoon. Sonata 12 for two violins
and trombone. [etc.]
    1. Chamber music. 2. Trio-sonatas. I. Series.
Recent researches in the music of the baroque era ;
v. 23-24.
M2.R238 vol. 23-24 [M178] 77-11128
ISBN 0-89579-090-4 (set)

Contents

SELECTED ENSEMBLE SONATAS
Sonatas from *Sonate concertate*, Book II (1629)

Sonata 7
for Treble Instrument and Bassoon

30

Adagio

Sonata 11
for Two Treble Instruments and Trombone

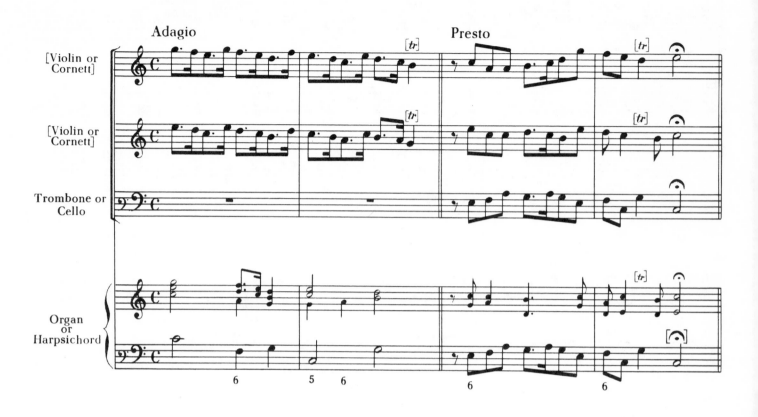

20 Adagio

Adagio

Molto adagio

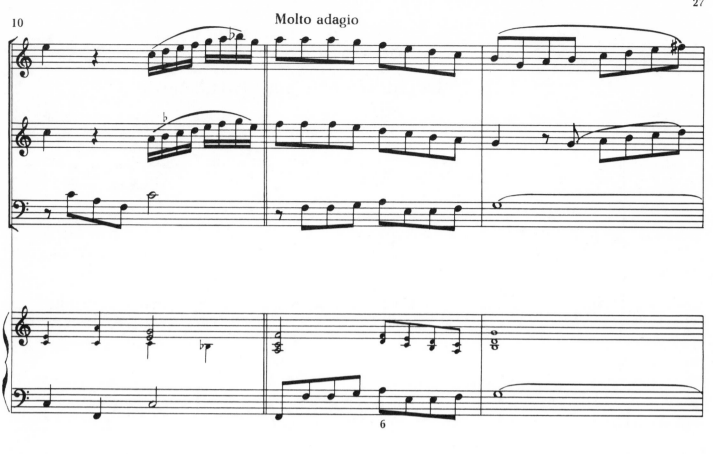

Sonata 12
for Two Treble Instruments and Trombone

(a) Could be played as:

Adagio

Allegro

35

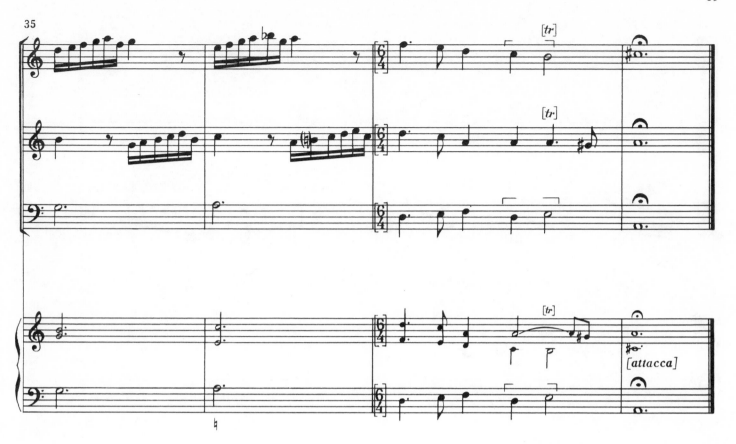

[Moderato]

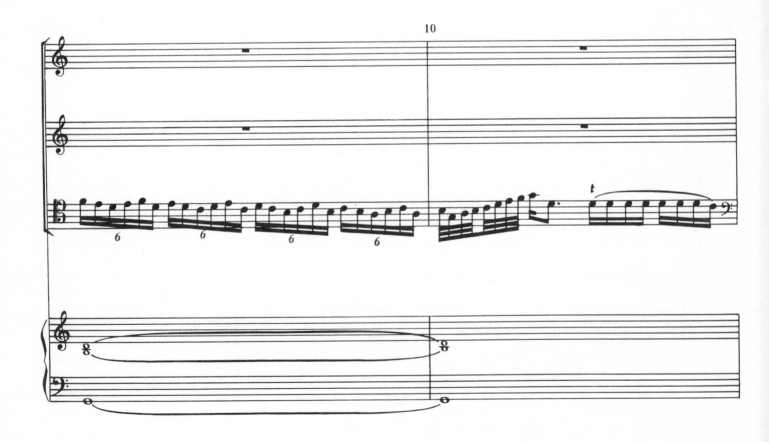

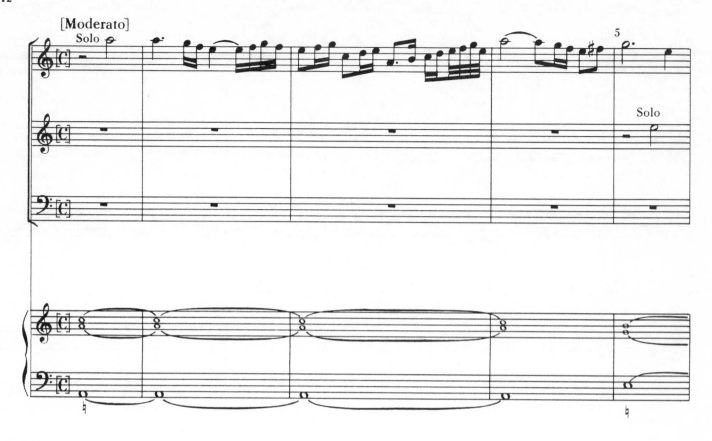

Sonata 15

for Bowed Instruments

(a) Appropriate viols may be substituted for the stringed instruments.

Allegro

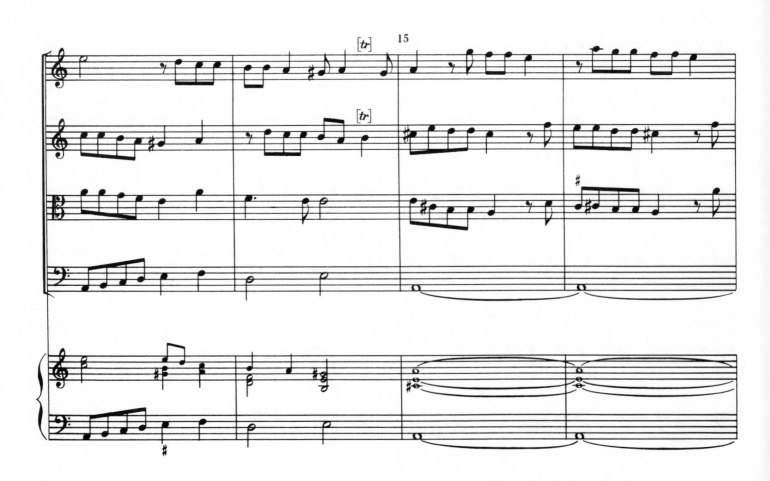

Allegro

Adagio

Adagio

Sonata 16
for Bowed Instruments

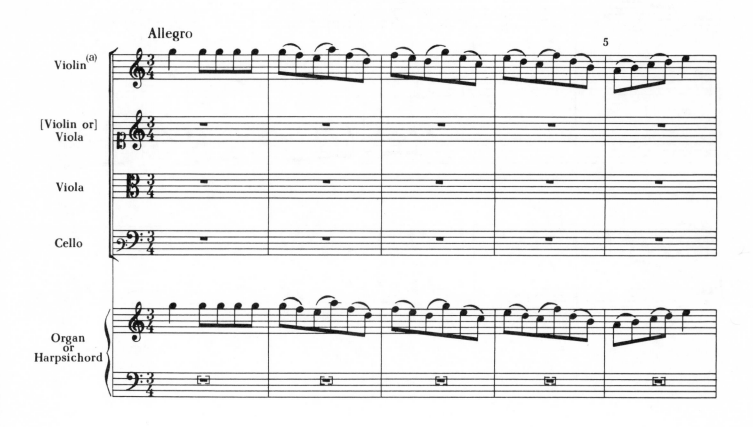

(a) Appropriate viols may be substituted for the stringed instruments.

[Allegro]

Adagio

10

15

[Allegro]

20

Adagio

Adagio

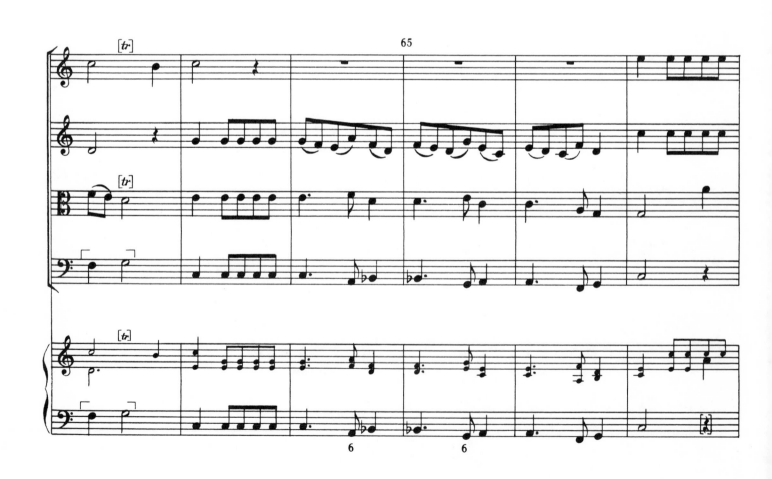

80

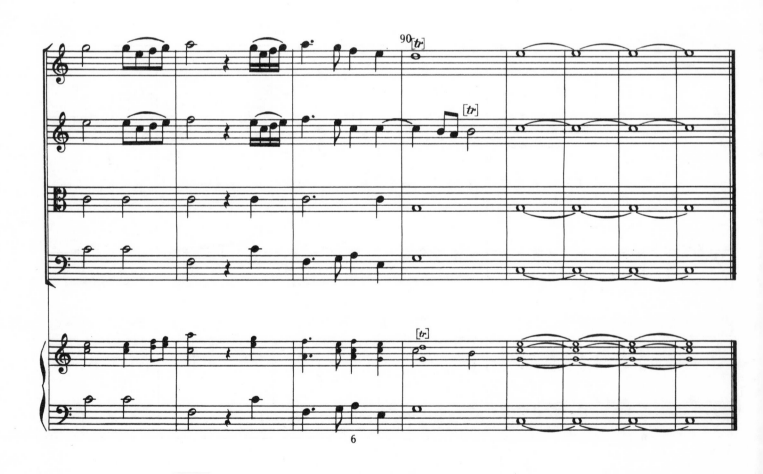

Sonata 17
For Cornett and Violin with Replying Cornett and Violin

(a) See the preface for a discussion of the use of the original continuo and of the double bass.

[Moderato: Tempo rubato]

[Allegro]

10

Vn.

Repl. Vn.

[sempre forte]

Solo echo

[sempre piano]

Eco: Va sonata il basso solo fino al duo

[Double bass only]

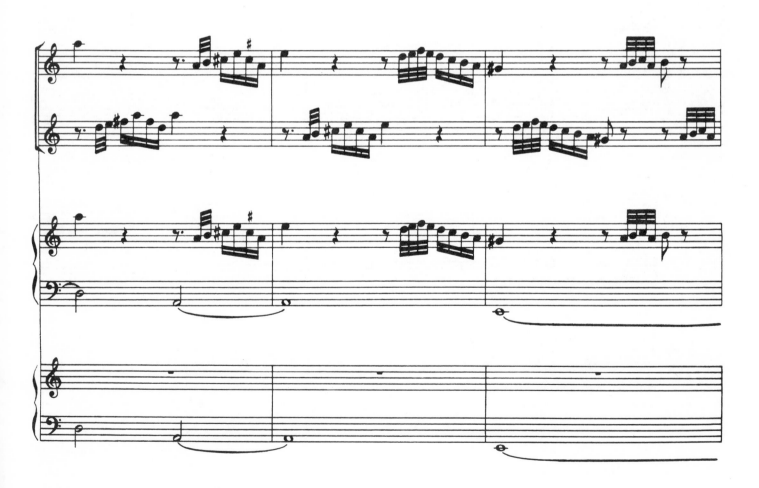

Presto

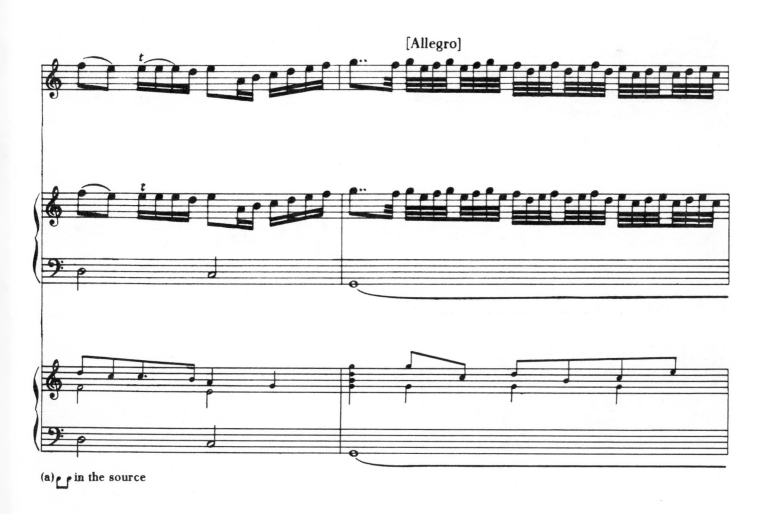

(a) ♩♩ in the source